THiS BOOK BELONGS TO

BONUS

Get your Free 50 Coloring Pages

On the Last Page!!

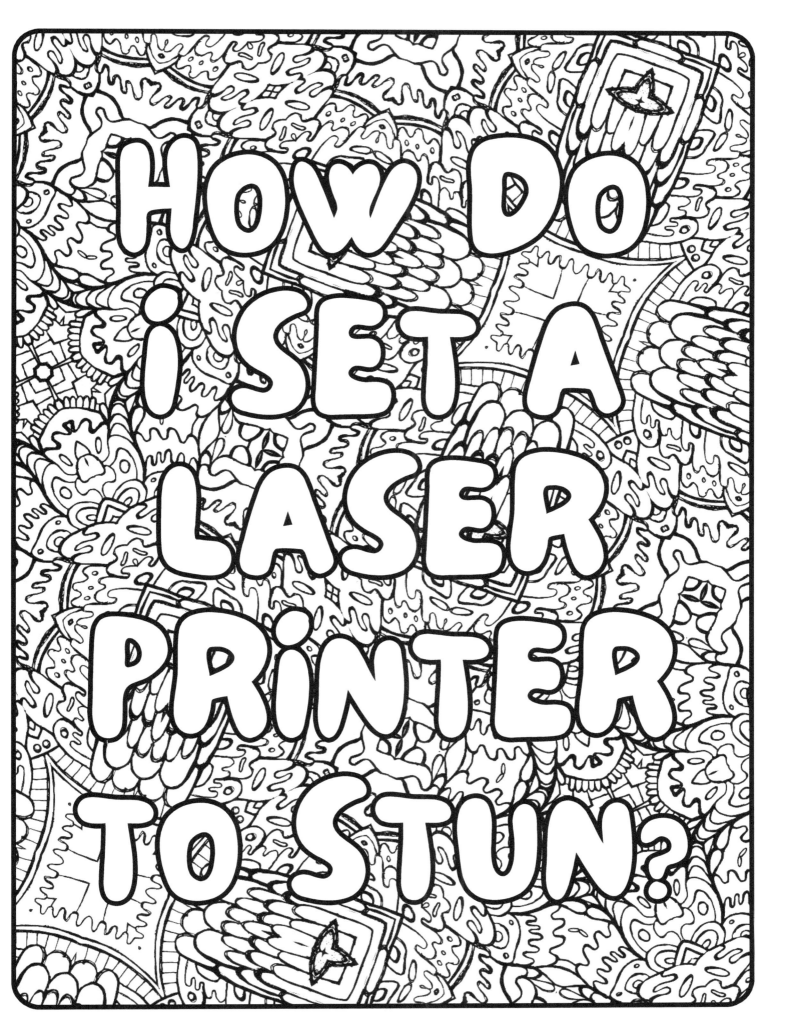

AHHHH... i SEE THE SCREW-UP FAIRY HAS VISITED US AGAIN.

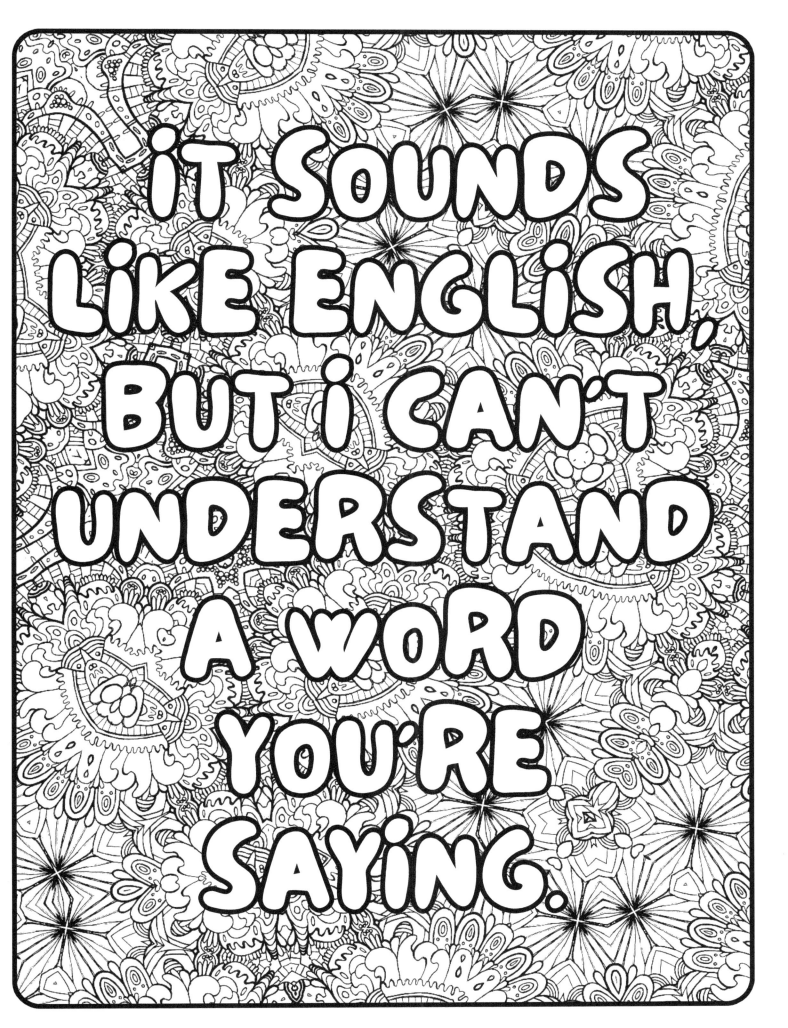

I SEE YOU'VE SET ASIDE THIS SPECIAL TIME TO HUMILIATE YOURSELF IN PUBLIC

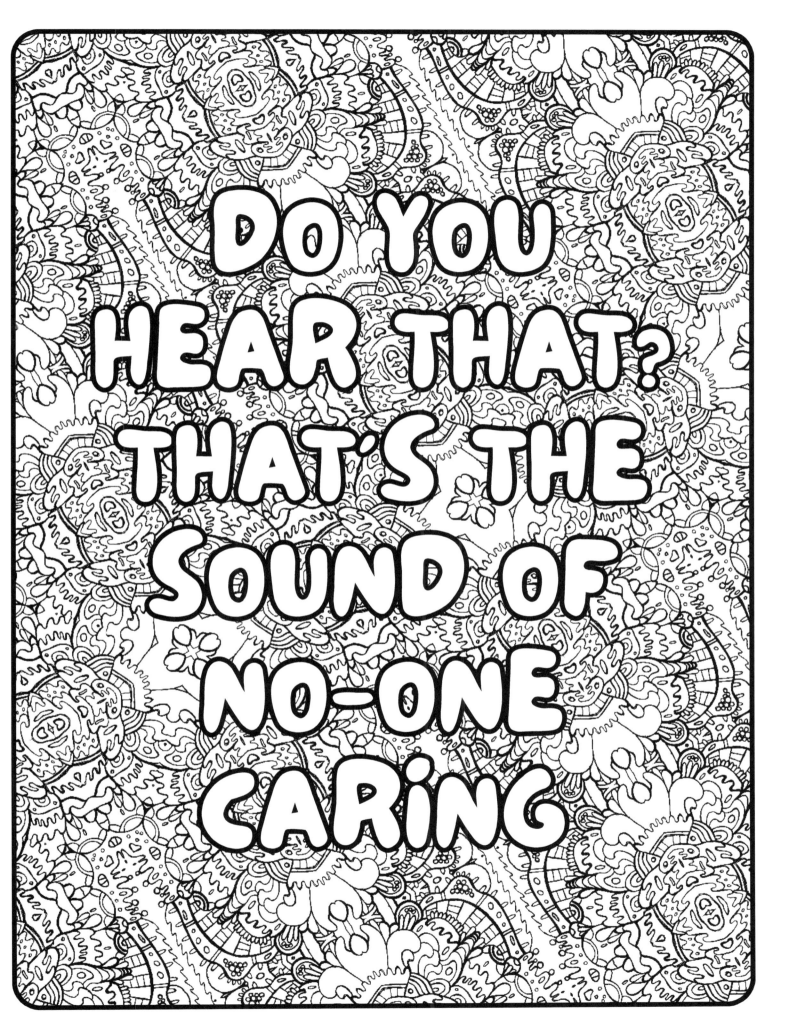

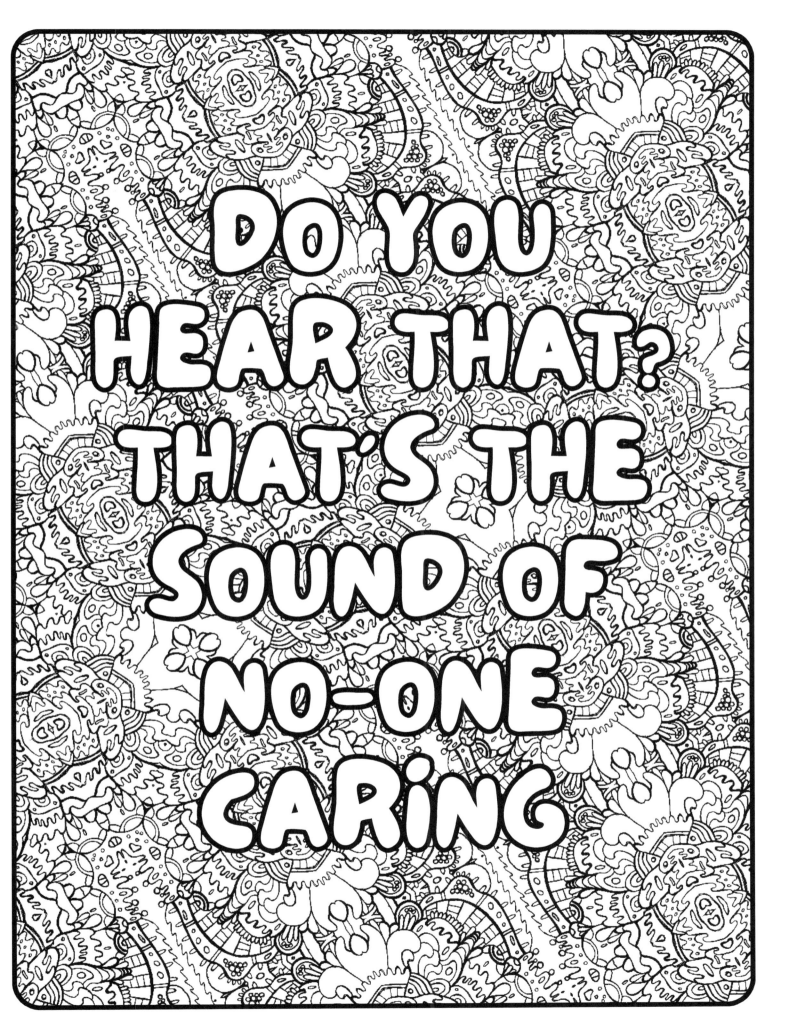

THANK YOU FOR YOUR PURCHASE

Scan the QR Code to Get your Free Coloring Pages